MARVEL

# SPIDER-MAN

# PHONICS COLLECTION

## Short Vowels

Scholastic Inc.

ISBN 978-1-338-74690-7

10 9 8 7 6 5 4 3 2 1      21 22 23 24 25

Printed in the U.S.A.   40

First printing 2021

Book design by Two Red Shoes Design

# A New Man

This story is filled with lots of short -a words, which appear in bold type. Here are some for you to sound out.

| | | |
|---|---|---|
| backpack | grabs | lab |
| bad | hand | lands |
| cash | hang | man |
| class | has | |

Peter Parker **has class** today.
He carries a **backpack**.

His **class** goes to a **lab**.

A spider **lands**
on his **hand**!
It bites.

Peter **hangs** from walls.

His **hands** shoot webs!

He is Spider-**Man**!

A **bad man grabs cash.**

# Peter stops the **man**.

Peter is a new **man**!

# Friends Are the Best

This story is filled with lots of short -e words, which appear in bold type. Here are some for you to sound out.

| | | |
|---|---|---|
| best | melt | them |
| everywhere | men | weather |
| friend | ready | web |
| get | sending | wreck |
| help | set | yes |
| jet | step | |

Bad **weather**!
Spider-Man **gets**
his **web ready**.

He looks **everywhere**.
A bad guy is **sending**
the snow.

Bad **men get set** to **wreck** the city.

Spider-Man **webs them**. The **men step** on the **webs**.

**Yes!**
**A jet!**

Ant-Man **helps**.

Hot lights **melt**
the bad **men**.
They **get them**!

**Friends** are the **best**!

# Wicked Widow

**Book 3**
short -i

This story is filled with lots of short -i words, which appear in bold type. Here are some for you to sound out.

| | | |
|---|---|---|
| flips | is | wicked |
| hitches | it | will |
| hits | swing | win |
| in | villain | |

Spider-Man **swings in**.
**It is** Black Widow!

She **hitches** a ride.

Black Widow tries
to get **in**.

**It is** not
Black Widow!
**It is** a **villain**!

# The **villain is wicked**.

She **hits** a shield.

Friends **will** help!

The **villain flips**.

The friends **swing in**.
They **win**!

# Stop the Spots

This story is filled with lots of short -o words, which appear in bold type. Here are some for you to sound out.

| | | |
|---|---|---|
| cop | on | spots |
| dogs | pop | stop |
| drops | rob | top |
| hot | shocked | |
| lot | shot | |

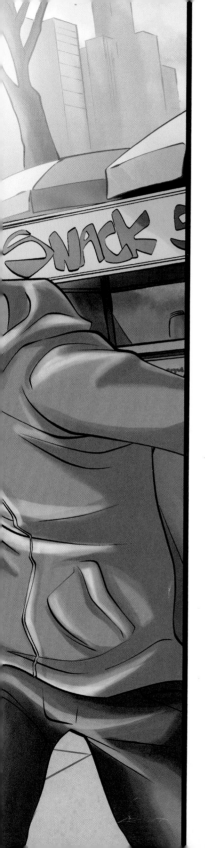

Peter and Gwen
**stop** for **hot dogs**.
Black **spots**
**rob** Gwen!

Spider-Man will **stop** the **spots**.

The **spots**
are **on top**.

Spider-Man **drops** in
**on** his friends.

They **pop** in
**on** a man with **spots**.

# The man is **shocked**.

He takes a **shot**.
He is blocked.

The friends **stop**
the man with **spots**!

# They find a **lot**.

# They call a **cop**.

Time for **hot dogs**!
They hit the **spot**.

# Just in Time

This story is filled with lots of short -u words, which appear in bold type. Here are some for you to sound out.

| | | |
|---|---|---|
| bucks | punches | uh-oh |
| fun | run | under |
| jump | some | up |
| must | thump | yum |

Miles and his friend
are at the zoo.

# Uh-oh!
## The animals run!

It is Rhino!
The guys **jump**
out of the way.

Spider-Man pulls
Rhino **up**.

**Thump**!
Rhino pushes
Spider-Man.

Miles **must** put on his spider suit.

Miles **punches** Rhino. Spider-Man gets **under** Rhino.

Rhino **bucks**.
They tie him **up**.

**Yum**!
Time for **some**
food and **fun**!

# Short Vowels Activities

The following pages contain activities to practice comprehension of short vowel sounds. As you go through the activities with your child, encourage them to sound out the words and say their answers out loud.

## Match up!

Spider-Man and Miles Morales match. Use your finger to draw a line to match the rhyming pairs.

| | |
|---|---|
| cash | lab |
| pan | tack |
| grab | bash |
| bad | mad |
| back | fan |

## Peter's Backpack

Peter Parker is going on a class trip! Help him pack his backpack by pointing to the short -a words in the box below.

pencil      cash

map      sock

shoe      pants

book

snack

gum

# Red Is Best!

Spider-Man probably loves the color red. It is a short -e word. Point to all the short -e words you see on this page.

| web | blue | ten | need |
|-----|------|-----|------|
| class | men | give | fight |
| guy | run | make | try |
| set | time | help | mess |
| leap | up | pet | best |

Help Spider-Man get ready for his next adventure!
Read each sentence with the short -e word that
best completes it.

| men | left | web | help |
|-----|------|-----|------|

Someone is in trouble.

Send _____!

Look _____ and right.

Watch out for the bad

_____.

Shoot that _____!

# Fix That Mix!

Look at the mixed-up short -i words below. Unscramble them to help Black Widow on her next mission.

gnwis

ihsw

pilf

inw

stiiv

# Word Stop!

Stop the man with spots by pointing to all the words that have the short -o sound.

| fly | stop | pop | man |
| --- | --- | --- | --- |
| bad | take | grab | fast |
| run | cop | shock | shot |

# Hot Dog!

Use your finger to trace a circle around the words that rhyme with "hot" and a square around the words that rhyme with "dog."

pot          lot

rot          dot

hog          jog

not

log

fog

# Buck Up!

Spider-Man fights Rhino. Use your finger to write and complete the short -u words below. Read each word out loud to help him with his moves.

p__nch          st__n

pl__s           j__mp

tr__ck          r__n

b__ck

## Word Hero

Help Spider-Man catch the villains by pointing to all the short-vowel words below.

May        Try

Man        Hit

Bad        Mix

Melt       Stop        Jump

Mean       Foe         Run

Friend     Shot        Beauty

## Group Review

Think about the short vowel sound each letter makes below. Use your finger to match each short vowel letter to words that contain that same short vowel sound.

| A E I O U |
| :---: |

pot             up

flag            grab

fit             weather

mud             lift

flop            best

## Short Vowel Sort

Use your finger to trace a line between words with the same short vowel sounds.

| | |
|---|---|
| dash | jump |
| web | hill |
| slid | apple |
| drop | men |
| club | frog |

## Super Sentences

Use each word below to create your own story. Use at least one other word with the same short vowel sound in each sentence. Try to make your sentences Super Hero–themed!

mad

ten

win

pop

fun

# You Did It!

Now you know your short vowel sounds. Read these stories again and again for even more super phonics fun! You'll be reading like a Super Hero in no time!